Meennunyakaa
Blueberry Patch

Meennunyakaa
Blueberry Patch

Written and illustrated by
Jennifer Leason

Written and translated by
Norman Chartrand

THEYTUS BOOKS
schchechmala children's series

Cataloguing in Publication information available from Library and Archives Canada

ISBN 978-1-926886-58-9 (hardcover)

Library of Congress Control Number: 2019936376
Simultaneously published in Canada and the United States in 2019

Summary: The story of how Indigenous people harvested berries
and how that tradition continues to this day.

MIX
Paper from
responsible sources
FSC® C016245

We acknowledge the support of the Canada Council for the Arts, which last year invested $157 million to bring the arts to Canadians throughout the country. Nous remercions le Conseil des arts du Canada de son soutien. L'an dernier, le Conseil a investi 157 millions de dollars pour mettre de l'art dans la vie des Canadiennes et des Canadiens de tout le pays. We acknowledge the support of the Province of British Columbia through the British Columbia Arts Council.

BRITISH COLUMBIA ARTS COUNCIL
Supported by the Province of British Columbia

Canada

Le Conseil des Arts du Canada | The Canada Council for the Arts

Cover and interior artwork by Jennifer Leason

Theytus Books
theytus.com

Printed and bound in Canada.

22 21 20 19 • 4 3 2 1

*This book is dedicated to our family and all the
Elders and language speakers who continue to share
the stories and memories of our ancestors.*

*For Dr. Gregory Younging. Thank you for being
a wonderful teacher, mentor, and friend.*

My story begins at blueberry-picking time, in the late 1940s, at Duck Bay near Camperville, Manitoba. Usually I'd be off hunting birds with my slingshot to make a crow-egg omelette, but today I was helping my family get ready for our two-day trip to the blueberry patch. We packed the horses and brought them to be hitched to our wagon. Most of our belongings were in the wagon, strapped down with rope.

May-abee kam-nee poon na kemint 1940's, me-ima Camperville Manitoba me-ima ya ne-ti-bache-quam ma-chis-hick ne-mound-do-na-mim-ka-kima kol-go ka-winaachee do-wang mista-tim-mook-o-kea-oma-up pim-now-wom weg-api-agoc pim-esee-yak ka-no-chee-ya-gog ne-pas-queb-poonag pem-esee gee-som-na-mick me-ashee a-mom-gong no-guma-thess gum-nob-snick-aposh tass-see-wat ne-nesch-ing je-nee pa-ang je-pa-awa-yeti meenum ka-nit ta-ig-ging blueberry patch

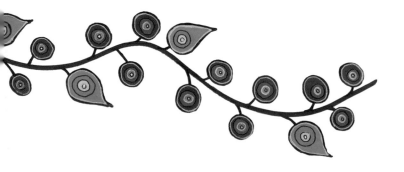

Our one-room house in Duck Bay looked very lonely after it was boarded up with planks, but we would be gone for a month. We said goodbye to our home and set out. I knew I would find new adventure and new friends. Our neighbours had also packed and were ready for the trip. Their horses were harnessed to their wagon. We were joined by other wagons to form a wagon train. We travelled in a line, heading toward the horizon where the river met the road, away from the lake. We were on our way to find the blueberries.

Tap-pis-ko-ne-wa-ki-gum-eman azaqumda tung ka-kum-na wasem-e-qumum shee-go esh-kom-dam okee-kepot-tum-na-wa ka-wap-mee-go dee-ma-man-me wa-ki-qum-nee-man mee-me macha-nim-dis-sha-mim yeti-kam-nee-kaa-ka-kee ishi-ang chee-wa-pa-dam mang-yech kaw-ween-na-ka-ka-ke ishang kec-ween-mowa-asha-ke kesh-shee ta-wag as-ha-mee-da wa-ma-gun-nee-yang asha mis-ta-tim-mook ke-onapisowak ka-kin-iga ota-pam-na-kook kee-ma-ja-ta-gass so-wuck ka-kima-gee-ma-cha-nim yeti cee-gee ka-na-kess-ka-wat-yec mee-ka-ma nee-mach-ja-num ema-on-jee-sai-quan che-me-kum-mang-eemee-wa mee-num

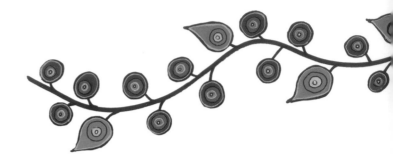

I hung on tight to the ropes in the wagon as it bounced up and down along the bumpy road. The iron rims of the wheels clanged against the stones. We had a team of two to pull the wagon. One was named Dick, and he was a mule. He was dark brown with long ears, and he was stubborn! Dick had a bad habit of sitting down and refusing to pull the wagon. The other horse was named Socks, because he looked like he had a pair of white socks on his feet. His rear was white, and he had a streak of white on his face. He was the king, and Dick was the dwarf.

A-nee-kook gee-mim-jim-ee ma-ota-pan-ac-kong kee-kosh-kay-shim-miss-see-yay pee-yob-bibk-shee-go assin-eek-ka-pen-na-ka-kee-imit-ta-kook neesh mista-tim-nook pess-sick Dick kee-is-im-nee-kas-shoo agita mista-tim agita-ka-kon-eta-egat mista-tim-oose Dick mish-ga-ti-sit me-kai-ishi-ma mut-ta-pit ka-wim-wee-ko-gim-ma-see-eni ota-pan-na-koom-awa mista-tim waba-sh-ki-a-zee gan-num-ka pee-sa-ka-wat o-tee-ke-wa-gis-ka-mee ta-koo-os-kul-tick ween-okima-shee-go Dick keg-a-gashee

That first day we travelled across the bridge, away from the gravel road, and started on a wagon trail through the bush and into new territory. What a great feeling to be going somewhere you have never been before! We stopped to camp by a big, open meadow that extended as far as the eye could see. The grass was long, and a creek about two feet wide and two feet deep, with clear, fast-flowing water, ran through the middle of the meadow. It was getting to be late afternoon as people unloaded their wagons and set up their tents.

Ka-ma-cha-ang-ke-asho-ga-mim cee-bee-ke-ma-kut-ta-mim-kun-ma ke-ma-ka-mim-iwa no-pee-ming-ima-ka-nee-ka ka-kee-ash-ay-amo ob-ji-ke-ne-man-dum-chee-isha-ima-ka-nee-ka ka-kee-ish-ang ke-kee-pish-chee-mim-che cha-pash-e-yang-im-ki-chee-mis-go-chee-ming show-wung-nom ta-ko-pa-kisg-mong-ena-ka-kech ka-kecg-oo-ke-gee-wsa-bum-da-seem-im-ma-mim-mig-chee-wa-ba ching-gai-ya-um kee-kum-mob-ye-gum-oom-em-ya nyis-cho-see bee-bee-kee-ti-mee ke-me-moch ewan-mow-way-ee-ima-ya-i-mis-go-shing asha-kee-nee-tee-pick ka-kim-ma-awe-ya-ke-osh-iga-wack

We cut tall grass to use as bedding in the tents. The horses munched on the grass, their tails swishing back and forth to fend off the horseflies and mosquitoes. I played with the other children. We played our hearts away. I felt like a high-flying nighthawk. The nighthawks would swoop down on our camp, making a farting noise as they flew. We called them nighthawk farts!

Emee-yech-ka-ka-gom-na-king mish-koss-cee-yung-o-kee-keesh-kis-ham-na-wan-chee apishe-mow-wung-agi-nee-pa-yang mista-tim-mook o-meech-im-ma-wa-emi-yay mis-koss-cee-yong oshoo-o-wan-ashhok-otis-yeb-pim-ma-wam ak-quay-shog-yat-wat-im-ne-wa ma-jin-no-shum-ka-kwa-tum-com-equat ag-im-moch-i-yak ke-we-chi-o-tum-mim-mo-mack ta-piss-eko-oke-yaa-ka-pam-e-piss-so-wat pess-quay ke-im-mam etis-a-pa-mach-eyam-speem-ink a-yee-kee-ish-ne-kan-nan-an piss-quay poo-kit-tim!

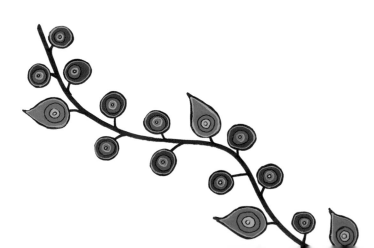

The bannock, cooked over red-hot coals, tasted so good with the clear, fresh water from the stream. The water tasted sweet, and I could smell the sharp fragrance of the cut grass and the smoke from the smudge, which filled the air.

Pa-quish-e-gum ke-kess-sig-assi-ima-unji sh-goo-ten-ing-agi-chee-kee-ween-ne-pa-kosh-ee yeti-ta-go-neg-nee-ima-unji-cee-bee-sing nee-bee-ke-ween-ne-pa-kut gee-nim-mam-clan-mis-ko-see-ka-kee-mani pe-to-wat-chee apish-emo-wang mim-nu-wum ke0nimo-na-kut-yea-ka-ke-cha-chiss-um-no-wat-ka-ek-yay mista-mook je-amook-go-wat sa-ke-mem-wasa-ke-gee-mum-nan-da-n-yech-scoot-tay

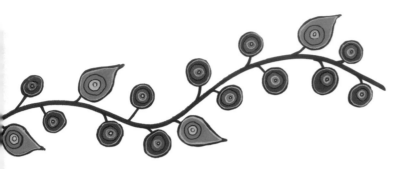

The day had to end, even though I was too tired and hyper to sleep. I lay in the canvas tent between my two brothers, Marcel and Hubert, feeling protected by the closeness of their bodies. I was thinking about all the fun we'd had that day. I could hear the men and women talking and laughing around the crackling fire. They were talking about the blueberries and how plentiful they were in some areas of Duck Mountain, Manitoba. My thoughts returned to that day, wanting it never to end. Fun, fun, fun!

Ke-no-tash-in-ka-ween dosh-ke-kash-kit-to-seem-je-ne-pa-an now-wa-yee-kin-ima-neesh-neshee-wa-j-we Marcel et Hubert kee-kee-shoo-sa-ka-koo-me-sheem-ma-yak kee-no-da-wak-a-ka-kee-kit-to-wack-she-go a-papi-yut-mee-ima-ke-keta-pick-es-quotang mee-num-o-dash-e-dan-na-waa a-pee-chee-o-sham-mee-ima-too-mim-a-shee-sheep wa-je-wum nee-na-ka-day-um-dam-no-koom ka-weem-ka-nee-da-wen-da-sheen-dhee-kee-pit-tis-seck amo-tom-mimo-wan amo-tom-mino-wan amo-tom-mimo-wan

The next morning we woke up, packed the wagon, and continued our journey. The wagon train came to a place called my-tic-ano-chi-go-ki-ishi-git, which means "tree that grows weird." There was a big Jack pine that looked like four trees grown into one. Several pairs of shoes were nailed to its trunk!

Kee-kee-shop-ne-wanish-ka-mim ke-poss-tass-o-mim ota-bana-kook me-shee-go-chee-ke-wa-yong kee-do-kosh e-me-mim-ima (my-tic-ano-chi-go-ki-ishi-git) kee-nitch-ja-ya-cee-bees ki-chi-asis-e-go-ma-mun-chee ta-bish-ko-nee-wim-my-ticok-awa-pess-sick-mytic am-isi-make-ka-ta-a-kee-pe-mosh-e-wat o-kee-sag-ana-wa wat-o-muck-kisi-yom-ima-mitic-gong

We passed my-tic-ano-chi-go-ki-ishi-git and then another mudhole.
The wagons went one by one. We came to Pelican River, where someone had
made a ka-nap-ac-kos-ekat-dec, which is a bridge made of wooden planks.
This would be the camp for the blueberry pickers. People from Cowan and
other communities surrounding Duck Mountain all came together for this
month of the berries' ripening.

Ke-ke-pick-kon-mant my-tic-ano-chi-go-ki-ishi nina-ke-o-tita-mim ota-ga-na-kook-o-wee te-wat-je-aso-ga-wat ashi-jap-nee-ga-na-ke-ta-kosh-sahim-me-mim she-day-cee-bee-ima ka-nap-ac-kos-ekat-dec wood flooring bridge a-way-ak-a-kee-o-shut-toot my-tic-ash-ugum da-ke-shim-ne-mim-me-nun-ima-chee-ma wis-o-wum mis-so-ya am-mis-ima-chi-ke-ta-kish e-mook-a-gil-ma-wis-o-want Cowan da-koo-ek-yay-aki-aya-wat-pes-shoo-shee-sheep-wa-ji-wa

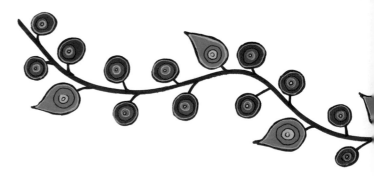

There were blueberries everywhere! This place was heaven for children. Little Jack pines grew in the sandy hills that stretched out for miles. In the distance there were larger Jack pines and poplar trees. We set up our tent and camped there for the month, until the blueberries were all gone.

Miss-yay-mee-num-ke-ta-ko-noom mee-oma-tag-is-ko-kit-chi-nish-i-go-mo agi-ke-om-shish-een-ima-chi-o-tum-mim-o-wang o-sis-ego-ma-ish-eek-kee-pe-mig-kee-yuk-mi-se-way me-ima-ka-pee-mig-nam-mee-mum me-ima-kee-o-shig-ke-wag me-ima-kay-a-ya0mim-min-ick mee-mum-chee-da-ko-kum-wee-gos-atick-gog

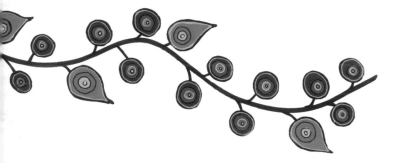

At the end of the month we packed up our wagon, joined the wagon train, and made our way back home to Camperville.

Mee-nun-ka-poo-niz-e-ging-ke-pos-tass-o-mim-chee kee-a-yang-yeti an-da-yang Camperville

Activities

1. What is the name of the mule that helped pull the wagon? What do you imagine he looked like? Draw a picture.

2. Make bannock in a cast-iron pan or on the stove (see next page for recipe).

3. What word does Elder Norman use to describe the sound a nighthawk makes? What other animal sounds remind you of a different sound?

4. At nighttime the children would lie in the tents and listen to the adults telling stories. Are there stories your parents or grandparents tell that you can remember?

5. Go berry picking. What edible berries grow where you live? What can be made from the berries? Can you find recipes to use your berries?

6. Elder Norman talks about my-tic-ano-chi-go-ki-ishi-git ("tree that grows weird"), where there was a big Jack pine that looked like four trees grown into one. Go for a walk and look at the trees. Do some trees look different than what you would expect?

7. Where in Manitoba are Duck Bay, Camperville, and Duck Mountain? Which Indigenous peoples reside in this area? Which treaties apply to this territory, and when were they established? What is a treaty?

Bannock

Ingredients

3 cups all-purpose flour
2 tablespoons baking powder
1 tablespoon sugar
½ teaspoon salt
½ cup margarine (or butter or shortening)
¾–1 cup of milk or water

Directions

* Mix together flour, baking powder, sugar, and salt.
* Work in the margarine with your hands until you've made a nice crumble.
* Gradually mix in enough milk or water to make a dough that is soft but not sticky. Knead.
* Shape into a ball, place on a cast-iron pan or greased baking sheet, and flatten into a circle about 1 inch thick.
* Bake at 425°F (220°C) for 25 minutes or until lightly browned.

Jennifer Leason (Keesis Sagay Egette Ekwe: First Shining Rays of Sunlight Woman) is Saulteaux-Métis Anishinaabek and a member of the Pine Creek Indian Band, Manitoba. She is the proud mother of two children, Lucas and Lucy. Jennifer is an assistant professor in Indigenous Peoples' Health at the University of Calgary and holds a PhD (University of British Columbia) and BA (University of Saskatchewan).

Norman Chartrand is Saulteaux-Métis Anishinaabek. He is Jennifer's great-uncle and the son of Elise Beauchamp and Arthur Jacque (Jimmy) Chartrand. Elise Beauchamp was the daughter of Philoméne Klyne and Jean Beauchamp (son of Nancy Chartrand and Joseph Beauchamp). Arthur Jacque Chartrand was the son of Julia Brass (daughter of Julia McLeod of Pelly and George Brass) and William Gédeon Chartrand (son of Sophie Genaille and William Chartrand). He is a member of the Pine Creek Indian Band, Manitoba.

For those who are interested in listening to the story told in Anishinaabemowin by Elder Norman Chartrand, please visit www.jenniferleason.com.

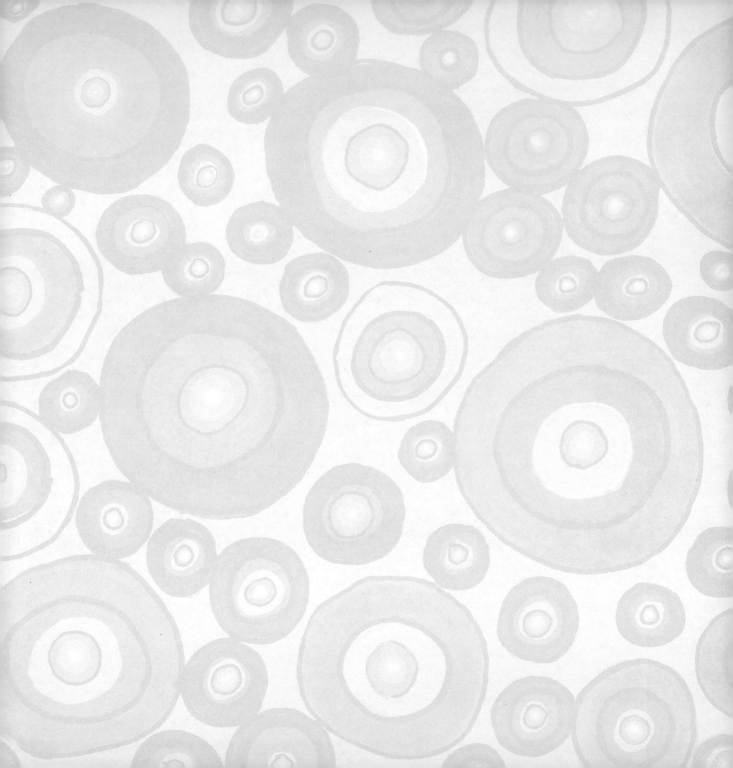